OUR CAT
SMUDGE

Judith Byron Schachner

CAT'S Whiskers

THE WATTS PUBLISHING GROUP LTD

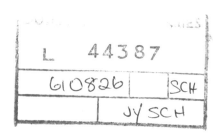
This edition first published in 2000 by
Cat's Whiskers
96 Leonard Street
London EC2A 4XD

ISBN 1 90301 223 6 (hbk)
ISBN 1 90301 224 4 (pbk)

First published in the United States under the title THE GRANNYMAN
by Judith Byron Schachner
Copyright © 1999 by Judith Byron Schachner
UK text copyright © Cat's Whiskers 2000
Published by arrangement with Dutton Children's Books,
a division of Penguin Putnam Inc.

A CIP catalogue record for this book is available from the British Library.

Printed in Belgium.

Smudge was a very old cat.

Apart from his nose, the rest of him had stopped working properly a long while ago. He was blind and he was deaf, and his bones creaked when he climbed up the stairs.

But his family loved him dearly, and did everything they could to make him comfortable in his old age.

Smudge had no teeth left, and mealtimes were messy.
Smudge didn't like the bib he had to wear, nor the
baby food that he was fed.

But he loved to be warm. He found hot spots all over the house, and stretched and basked and baked until he was almost too hot to touch.

At night he sometimes slept in one of the beds.
The family loved him so much, they didn't mind that
he was a bit smelly.

On other nights Smudge would stay awake in the comfortable armchair, and shuffle through a lifetime of old memories.

Smudge could still remember just after he was born.
There were lots of other kittens that looked like him.

One by one, the kittens went off to new homes.
All except him. Nobody seemed to want him.
He was so small.

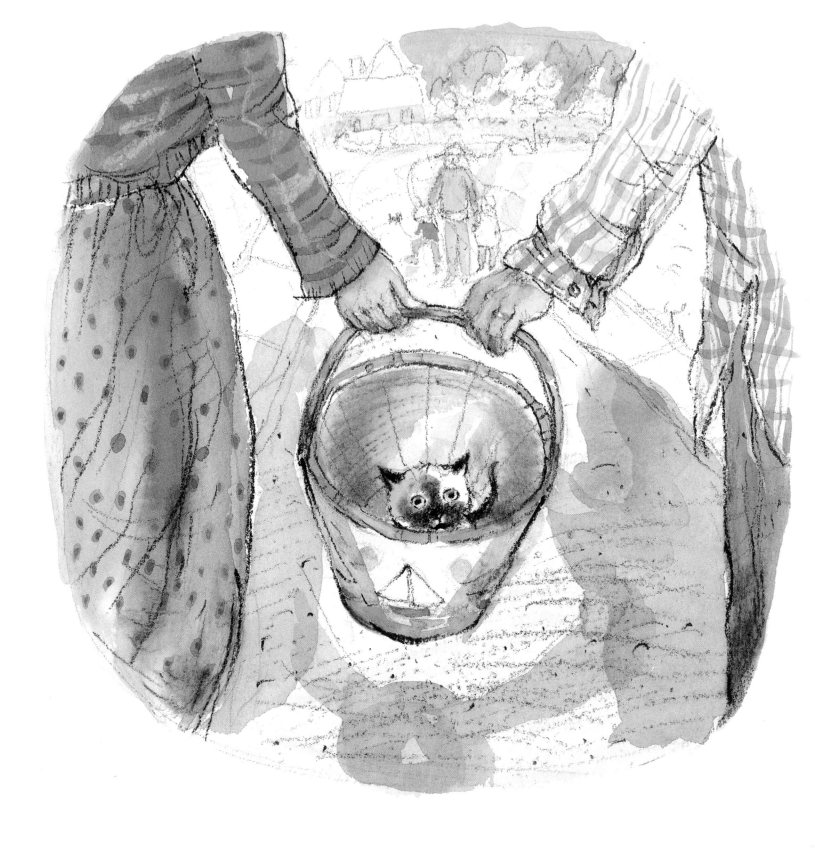

And then, one day, a nice couple came along and liked him. They put him in a bucket and carried him to their home. They called him Smudge.

Smudge loved being a kitten. He climbed, he clawed, he chased, he chewed everything in sight.

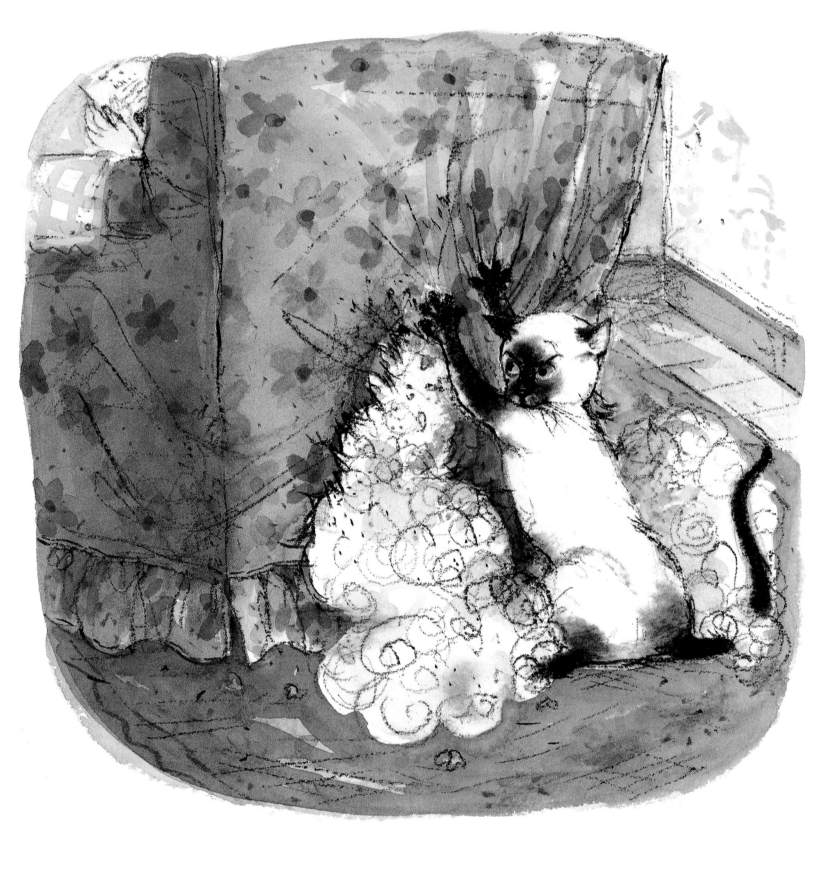

He used the backs of chairs to make beautiful woolly sculptures - until his claws were clipped.

As he grew up, he learned how to help around the house.
He tidied the plants with his teeth...

and dusted under
the cupboards.

Smudge's family got bigger, and so too did his
responsibilities. Two young ones arrived; Smudge
had to teach them how to be good cats.

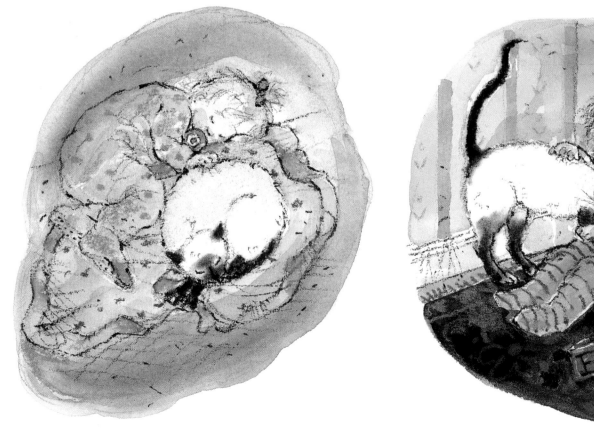

In his middle age, Smudge discovered the joys of music.
He played the piano, and occasionally sang solos at midnight.

Sometimes, when he was in the mood, he became a big game hunter.

Smudge's life had been so full.

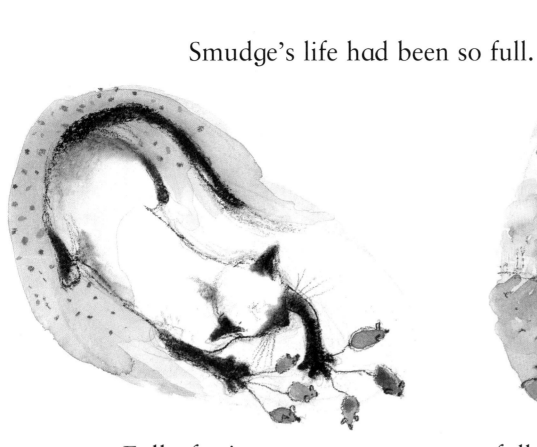

Full of mice,

full of hisses,

full of hugs,

and full of kisses.

But now things were different. Smudge felt he wasn't needed any more, and that his family's kindness was just pity.

One night, feeling totally useless, Smudge stuck his
bony old legs into the air and breathed his last.

Or so he imagined... But a few seconds later, something soft was plopped onto his tummy.

Smudge sniffed to the left and sniffed to the right. Why, it's a little kitten, he thought. Even though it had been years ago, he remembered how he had helped the other new pets when they had come into the house. He wondered if he could still do it.

With great difficulty, Smudge climbed down from his chair and carried the kitten downstairs to a fresh saucer of milk.

Then he showed the kitten how whiskers should be cleaned. The kitten did his best to imitate the old cat.

But when Smudge twitched his tail, the kitten leaped onto his head, expecting a ride around the room. Smudge was not pleased.

After a while, Smudge led the kitten over to his box. It took so long for the kitten to heap a mountain of litter onto the floor that Smudge had a little nap.

When he awoke, the kitten had gone. Smudge hobbled back upstairs to the armchair, to sit alone in a sliver of moonlight. It must have been a dream...

Or so he thought.

Just then, something small and soft jumped on top of him. Smudge sniffed to the left and sniffed to the right. Why, it's my kitten, he thought.

Smudge began to give the kitten a bath. He washed his little ears and licked his little nose. He groomed his skinny tail and cleaned between each of his teeny-tiny toes. Then a grumbly-rumbly purr stirred deep within his chest, and he curled himself around his little pet.

And, as the days came and went, Smudge found a new sort of happiness and a new kind of strength in tenderly caring for his kitten. He was needed again.

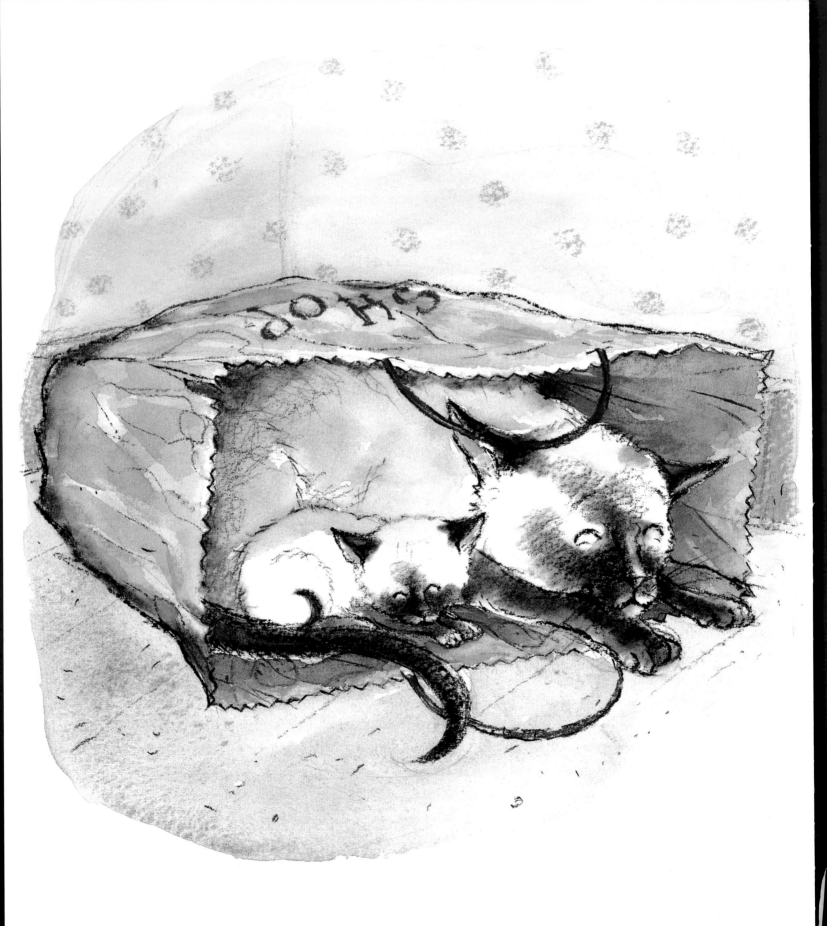

Life was worth living after all.